A GIFT FOR:

....

FROM:

....

How to Use Your Interactive Story Buddy™:

1. Activate your Story Buddy™ by pressing the "On / Off" button on the ear.
2. Read the story aloud in a quiet place. Speak in a clear voice when you see the highlighted phrases.
3. Listen to your Story Buddy™ respond with several different phrases throughout the book.

Clarity and speed of reading affect the way Scooby-Doo™ responds.
He may not always respond to young children.

Watch for even more interactive Story Buddy™ characters.
For more information, visit us on the Web at Hallmark.com/StoryBuddy.

TM & © Hanna-Barbera.
(s12)

This edition published in 2012 by Hallmark Gift Books,
a division of Hallmark Cards, Inc.,
Kansas City, MO 64141
Visit us on the Web at Hallmark.com.

Editor: Emily Osborn
Designer: Mark Voss
Art Director: Kevin Swanson
Production Artist: Dan Horton

ISBN: 978-1-59530-469-8
PSB2118

Printed and bound in China
APR12

I Reply ™ TECHNOLOGY

Hallmark's **I Reply Technology** brings your Story Buddy™ to life! When you read the key phrases out loud, your Story Buddy™ gives a variety of responses, so each time you read feels as magical as the first.

BOOK 1

SCOOBY-DOO!

WHO ARE YOU?

Hallmark

GIFT BOOKS

BY ANDRE DU BROC • ILLUSTRATED BY RICHARD LAPIERRE

It was a beautiful spring day in Coolsville. The Mystery Inc. gang had just arrived at the annual Pet Adoption Party in Coolsville Park. There were dogs and cats. There were birds and hamsters. There were even goldfish in little bowls. And in the middle of it all, a chef was grilling hamburgers for lunch. Yum!

Fred, Daphne, Velma and Shaggy each got a burger for lunch. Shaggy was extra hungry, so he bought two. But just when they opened their mouths to take a bite, they heard a loud noise.

"Jinkies! What was that?" asked Velma. The gang put down their burgers to peek around the corner. But there was nothing there.

When they walked back toward their lunch, Shaggy's burger was gone!

"Well, it didn't just disappear!" Velma said. "Maybe there's a burger bandit."

"Or a ghost!" said Daphne.

"Zoinks!" cried Shaggy. He didn't like ghosts. Especially ghosts that stole people's lunch.

"Well, gang," said Fred. "It looks like we've got a mystery to solve!"

Fred, Velma, and Daphne all split up
to look for the mysterious burger bandit.
Shaggy stayed to finish his lunch.

He kept his eyes wide open
as he unwrapped his last burger.
He slowly opened his mouth
to take a big bite and . . .

CHOMP!

Shaggy was nose to nose with a big brown dog!
"You must be the burger bandit!" Shaggy chuckled,
patting the dog between his large, pointy ears.

The dog smiled and licked Shaggy's face.

"Are you still hungry?" Shaggy asked his new friend. "I know I am!"

The dog's tummy began to rumble.

"Two more burgers, please!"
Shaggy called to the chef.

The man handed Shaggy a bag
of burgers and a box of dog treats.

hamburger......$1.75
cheeseburger......$1.50
veggie burger......$1.00
french fries......$1.00
fountain soda.....$1.00

"These are for you. And these are for your four-legged friend," he said.
"Wow, thanks!" said Shaggy.

"They're called SCOOBY SNACKS dog treats," said the chef. "Dogs will do just about anything for them."

"Really?" said Shaggy, reaching into the box. The big brown dog's face lit up when he saw Shaggy holding up a delicious Scooby Snack. "Sit!" said Shaggy.

The big brown dog zoomed
behind a tent and then zoomed
back with a folding chair.

He quickly unfolded it. Then he sat down.

"Wow!" said Shaggy. "I've never seen a dog sit like that!"

A crowd began to form around Shaggy and the amazing big brown dog.

The audience cheered loudly.

Shaggy gave the Scooby Snack to his new friend.
"I wonder what other tricks he can do," Shaggy thought to
himself. "Shake hands!" he said as he held up another treat.

The big brown dog then went to each person in the crowd
and shook their hands with his big brown paw.
Again the audience cheered loudly.

Soon Fred, Daphne, and Velma saw the big crowd. And they saw that Shaggy and the big brown dog were right in the middle! "Looks like our burger bandit wasn't a ghost after all," giggled Daphne.

"G-g-g-ghost?" said Shaggy.

"RI'm not a ghost!" said the big brown dog.

"Jinkies! He spoke!" Velma said.

Everyone gasped. The gang was amazed.

"ZOINKS!"

said Shaggy. "That was amazing! Do it again!"
But the big brown dog just looked at him.

"Wait! I know!" Shaggy grabbed the box of dog treats and pulled one out. "Would you do it for a Scooby Snack?"

"Rank you, Raggy!" the dog said, gobbling up the yummy snack.

"Like, wow!" said Shaggy. "This is the dog for me!"

"He does like you," said the woman from the adoption agency.

"But having a dog is a big responsibility. You'll have to take him for walks, give him baths, and feed him. And believe me, this dog can eat a lot!"

"That's okay," said Shaggy. "I can eat a lot, too!" Shaggy didn't mind doing a little extra work, because he knew this dog was special.

The gang smiled as they watched Shaggy adopt his new friend.
"Does he have a name?" Daphne asked.

"Well, he does love these snacks."
Shaggy patted the dog between his ears.
"How about we call him Scooby-Doo?"

The dog jumped up and wrapped his big front
paws around Shaggy's shoulders.
"Scooby-Dooby Doo!" He seemed to like it!

And everyone, especially Shaggy,
was happy to have such a great new friend.
Everyone in the crowd smiled as they watched
Scooby lick Shaggy's face.
The audience cheered loudly.

The four friends hugged the newest member of their mystery-solving gang and said, "Scooby-Doo, we love you!"

IF YOU HAVE ENJOYED READING WITH SCOOBY-DOO™, WE WOULD LOVE TO HEAR FROM YOU!

Please send your comments to:
Hallmark Book Feedback
P.O. Box 419034
Mail Drop 215
Kansas City, MO 64141

Or e-mail us at:
booknotes@hallmark.com